Never
Follow a
DINOSAUR

Alex Latimer

Picture Corgi

For Lily and Isla

Tameside Libraries	
3 8016 0200 7055	
PETERS	11-Jul-2016
JF	£6.99
CEN	

PICTURE CORGI

UK | USA | Canada | Ireland | Australia
India | New Zealand | South Africa

Picture Corgi is part of the Penguin Random House group of companies
whose addresses can be found at global.penguinrandomhouse.com.

www.penguin.co.uk   www.puffin.co.uk   www.ladybird.co.uk

Penguin
Random House
UK

First published 2016
001

Printed in China
A CIP catalogue record for this book is available from the British Library

ISBN: 978–0–552–56938–5

All correspondence to:
Picture Corgi, Penguin Random House Children's,
80 Strand, London WC2R 0RL

MIX
Paper from
responsible sources
FSC® C018179
FSC
www.fsc.org

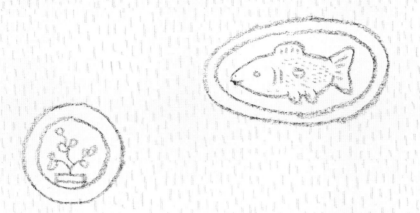

One afternoon, Joe and his sister Sally
spotted a strange set of footprints . . .

"Who do you think made those?" asked Sally.

Joe took a closer look.
"Hmmm, by the size and shape
I think they must certainly have been
made by a **dinosaur**."

They followed the footprints right up to Willoughby's bowl. It was empty.

"It must be a very **hungry** dinosaur," said Sally. "It has eaten all of Willoughby's food!"

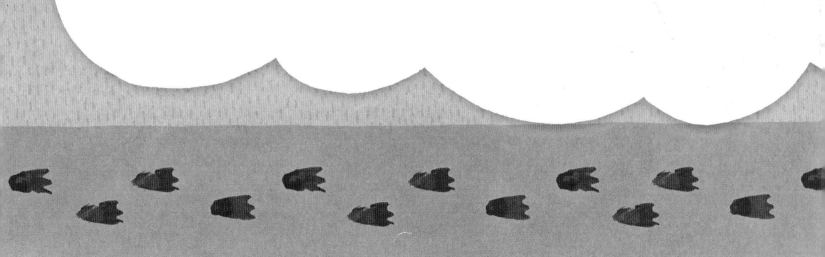

They followed the footprints
into the garden.

"Look how deep the footprints are here,"
said Joe. "It must be a very
heavy, **hungry** dinosaur to have
made such deep footprints."

grumble

The footprints carried on,
right through Dad's fish pond.

"It seems to like water," said Sally.
"So it's a **heavy**, **hungry**,
swimming dinosaur!"

grumble

A little further on, the footprints went
all squiggly and overlapping.

"What happened here?" asked Joe.

"Probably some sort of dance," said Sally.
"I'd say it's a **heavy**, **hungry**,
swimming, **dancing** dinosaur."

"What are all these leaves
doing here?" asked Sally.

"The dinosaur probably bumped
its head on that branch," said Joe.
"So it's a **hungry**, **heavy**,
swimming, **dancing** dinosaur
with a **headache**."

"And look, there are only right foot footprints here," said Sally.

"It must have hurt its left foot on this rock and hopped about in pain," said Joe. "So it's a **hungry**, **heavy**, **swimming**, **dancing** dinosaur with a **headache** and a **sore foot**."

grumble

And then, a little further along,
the footprints stopped altogether.

Sally and Joe looked around for
the **hungry**, **heavy**,
swimming, **dancing** dinosaur
with a **headache** and
a **sore foot** – but it was
nowhere to be seen.

grumble

They trudged home,
thinking of all sorts
of explanations.

But they didn't think
it had been hit by
a meteorite . . .

or magicked away
by a magician . . .

or taken by
aliens . . .

"You should **NEVER** follow a dinosaur," said Mum, when they got home. "Especially not a **hungry** one!"

"And it probably wasn't a dinosaur at all," added Dad. "Because they're extinct."

But Sally and Joe were convinced it really **WAS** a dinosaur.
And they were going to prove it.

"I know," said Sally. "Let's build a trap and catch it!"

So they spent all afternoon drawing and planning and building the perfect dinosaur trap.

THIS WAY FOR CAT FOOD

music for dancing

bath for swimming

And when they were done, they set the cat food in place and left it overnight.

The next morning, Sally and Joe ran out into
the garden to check their trap.

The bait was gone and there were footprints
leading right to the edge of the pit.

But
when they looked
into the hole there was
no dinosaur.

"How did it escape?" wondered Joe.
"It's not as though it can fly."

"But what if it can?" Sally shouted.
"What if it's a
hungry,
heavy,
swimming,
dancing dinosaur
with a **headache**
and a **sore foot**
and
WINGS!"

Both Sally and Joe looked up into the sky, and there,
flying above them, was the DINOSAUR!
It looked **very** hungry indeed.

grumble

"Uh-oh!"
said Joe.

"**Run!**"
yelled Sally.

grumble

But in no time the dinosaur had scooped them
up off the ground . . .

So you see, the reason you should **NEVER** follow a dinosaur is that some dinosaurs are just plain hungry.

But ...

luckily for Sally and Joe, once **this** hungry, heavy, flying dinosaur had soothed its headache and put a plaster on its sore foot, finished its dance, and had a refreshing swim – all it needed was . . .

. . . some help with cake baking!

So Sally and Joe helped the dinosaur to bake
– and eat – lots of delicious cakes. Phew!